BEAUTIFUL

BY SUSI GREGG FOWLER ❖ PICTURES BY JIM FOWLER

Greenwillow Books, New York

For George Chapman,
who walked in beauty

Acrylic paints were used for the full-color art.
The text type is Seagull Medium.
Text copyright © 1998 by Susi Gregg Fowler
Illustrations copyright © 1998 by Jim Fowler
http://www.williammorrow.com
Printed in Hong Kong by South China Printing Company (1988) Ltd.
First Edition   10 9 8 7 6 5 4 3 2 1

Library of Congress Cataloging-in-Publication Data
Fowler, Susi Gregg.
Beautiful / by Susi Gregg Fowler ; pictures by Jim Fowler.
p.   cm.
Summary: A young gardener and Uncle George collaborate
on a garden, so that when a very sick Uncle George comes
home from the doctor he is greeted with beautiful flowers.
ISBN 0-688-15111-6 (trade).   ISBN 0-688-15112-4 (lib. bdg.)
[1. Gardening—Fiction.   2. Uncles—Fiction.
3. Terminally ill—Fiction.]   II. Fowler, Jim, ill.   III. Title.
PZ7.F82975Bej   1998   [E]—dc21
97-6323   CIP   AC

Uncle George makes dark places bright and turns ordinary places into something wonderful. He is a gardener, and he takes care of gardens all over town.

"Come outside," Uncle George said to me on my birthday.
I followed him out the door, and he pointed to a cardboard
box next to the house. "There's your present."
I looked inside. There were gardening tools, a piece of wire
screen on a wooden frame, and some packages of seeds.

We worked all weekend putting in my garden.
Uncle George was a little tired, so I did all the
digging. He showed me how to shake the dirt
through the screen to get rid of the rocks, how
to poke my finger in the dirt to make a place
for the seeds, and how to pat the dirt back
over the seeds when the planting was done.
"I like gardening," I said.
"Beautiful," said Uncle George.

"Now what?" I asked.

"Now you take care of the seeds and wait
 for glory," he said.

"How do I take care of them?"

"Water them when the dirt feels dry and pull
 out any grass or weeds," said Uncle George.

"And don't forget to talk to them."

"Talk to them?"

"Yes," said Uncle George. "They like that.
 Cheer them on. Love them. I'll be back when
 they're ready to bloom."

"Where are you going?" I asked.

"I'm sick," said Uncle George, "and I need
   some care that I can't get here."

"I'll miss you," I said.

"That's why I want you to have your own
   garden this year," said Uncle George.

"Maybe you won't feel I'm so far away."

Every day I checked my seeds. Sometimes
I gave them water. Sometimes I just talked
to them. And when I was in the garden,
Uncle George did seem closer.

Uncle George sent me a postcard. "They like
it if you sing, too. Love, Uncle George."
"What on earth does that mean?" Daddy asked.
"I know," I said.
I ran outside and sang "My Bonnie
Lies Over the Ocean." Uncle George
likes that song, so I thought my seeds
would, too.

It seemed as if Uncle George had been gone a long time before anything happened. Maybe it's just because I missed him. Maybe it's just because I wanted my seeds to grow. But finally, one day, there were green things poking up out of the ground.

"Momma, look!" I yelled. "Can we call Uncle George?"

Momma agreed, but she said we'd have to keep it short.

When I talked to Uncle George, his voice was very soft.
"You keep talking and singing to those plants," he said.
"I expect blossoms when I get home. I knew you were
a gardener."

Once the plants started growing, they changed a bit every day. Soon there were little green knobs on the stems. Momma said they were leaves, but I couldn't tell. Then one day the knobs opened like tiny hands.

I drew a picture, and Momma sent it to Uncle George.

He sent back a postcard. It just said, "Beautiful."

In a few weeks there were buds all over my plants. Momma said that wherever there were buds, there would be flowers.

I called Uncle George again.

"Keep it up," he said. "I'm coming home in a few days."

"I'm glad Uncle George is almost well," I told Momma
when I got off the phone. "He'll be home soon."

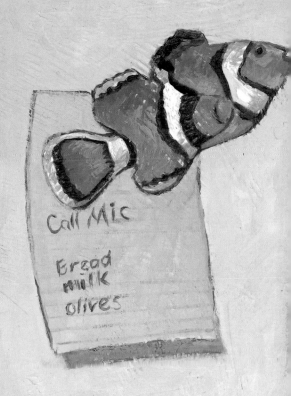

"Come here a minute," Momma said. She looked
sad. "We don't think Uncle George is going to get
well, honey," she said. "He's coming home, but he's
getting sicker. The doctors can't help anymore.
Now he just wants to be with us."
I started to cry.

"Here's the good news," Momma said. "He's going
   to move in with us. Can he have your room?"
"Sure," I said. "I'll sleep on the floor."
   Momma shook her head. "You'll have to stay in
   the baby's room."
   I made a face.
   I went out to my garden and talked to the plants.
"You must bloom soon," I said. "Uncle George is
   coming home."

When Uncle George got off the plane, I hardly
recognized him. He was very, very thin and wore
a knit cap over his head. Momma said he didn't
have very much hair anymore.
A strange lady pushed him toward us in a wheelchair.
I felt shy, but when he saw me, he smiled. His smile
looked the same as always, so I ran up and hugged
him.
"How's my favorite gardener?" he asked me.
"How's MY favorite gardener?" I said.

We went to get his baggage.
Uncle George kept licking his lips. He seemed
thirsty. "How are the flowers?" he said so quietly
I could hardly hear him.
"They're big," I said. "Wait until you see them,
Uncle George. Momma says they're almost ready
to bloom."
"Ready for glory," whispered Uncle George.
"Beautiful."

As soon as we got home, Uncle George
went to bed. He was too tired to look at
my garden. Two nurses came to the house
with some equipment, and Momma
asked me to go outside.
I went to the garden by myself.

Uncle George didn't even come to the table for dinner.
"I'll take his dinner in to him," I said.
Daddy shook his head. "Uncle George is just getting liquids now," he said. "It's easier for him than eating."

I didn't feel hungry anymore.
"I miss Uncle George the way
he used to be," I said.
Momma nodded.

The next morning I ran outside early to see my
plants. The buds were so big I could see the colors
trying to squeeze through the edges.
"There's orange and yellow and even some red
ones," I told Uncle George when he woke up.
"There are so many buds I can't even count
them, and they're starting to open."
Uncle George held my hand and smiled.
He didn't say "beautiful," but I could tell
he was thinking it.

He started to say something. I had to lean really close
to hear him. He stopped in the middle of a sentence
and looked at Momma standing in the doorway. He
seemed confused and kind of scared.

"It's okay, George," said Momma, taking his hand.
"You're just tired. Rest now."

Uncle George closed his eyes.

"We'll be right in the next room," Momma said.

The next day Uncle George didn't talk at all.
He slept almost all the time. I went in and
held his hand for awhile, but he didn't open
his eyes.

But the next day my flowers were blooming!
They were so beautiful I wanted Uncle
George to see them right away. I knew
he couldn't come outside.

I ran into the house. "Momma, they're blooming!
I have to pick some for Uncle George!"
Momma came outside with her garden scissors
and showed me how to cut the flowers so more
would grow back.

"Surprise," I said softly as I walked into my room.
  Uncle George opened his eyes, and I held out the
  flowers.
"Come here," he whispered.
  I walked over to him and gave him the flowers.
  He looked happier than he'd been since he came
  home.
"Don't go anywhere," Momma said.
"Okay." Uncle George laughed. It was a quiet,
  scratchy sound, but it was a laugh.
  Momma came back with her camera. "My favorite
  gardeners," she said. "Smile."
"Beautiful," said Uncle George.